In the golden evening sunlight, long ago, people meet to talk under the shade of a trailing fig tree.

The children gather around Mary. She is an old lady whom they love dearly, for she has a kind smile as she welcomes them all. "Mary, mother of Jesus, tell us your story," they ask.

And so she tells them the story they love to hear.

To Benedicta M.J.

To Theresa and Geoffrey, with love A.W.

First published in North America in 1999 by

Loyola Press

3441 North Ashland Avenue
Chicago, IL 60657

Originally published by Lion Publishing plc
Oxford, England

Text by Mary Joslin
Illustrations copyright © 1999 Alison Wisenfeld
This edition copyright © 1999 Lion Publishing

ISBN 0-8294-1380-4

Typeset in 16/27 Venetian
Printed and bound in Singapore
99 00 01 02 / 10 9 8 7 6 5 4 3 2 1

Mary
Mother
of Jesus

Mary Joslin

Illustrations by Alison Wisenfeld

Loyola Press
Chicago

"When I was a girl, I lived in a plain little town called Nazareth.
It stands among the hills of Galilee north of Jerusalem.
I remember so well one beautiful spring. The sky was blue, the
hillsides around were covered with wild flowers, and everything
in my life seemed sunny. I was nearly grown up, and my family
had arranged that I should marry a good man named Joseph—
Joseph the carpenter.

"Then, one day, there stood before me a bright and shining
figure: the angel Gabriel, with a message from God. 'Peace
be with you,' said Gabriel. 'God is with you, and has greatly
blessed you. God has chosen you to bear a child: God's own
Son. You must call him Jesus.'

"When I first heard this message, I was utterly dismayed; but I have always believed that God is the Wise One who made heaven and earth, and I know that God's plans are always good.

"I replied to the angel, 'I will do what God wants. May it happen to me as you have said.'

"Yet I knew that having a baby was going to turn my life upside down. To whom should I tell my news? Who would believe my story?

"I hurried off to visit my cousin, Elizabeth. She was expecting a baby, too. Everyone said it was a miracle, for in spite of being married many years, this was to be her first baby… and she was quite old.

"Elizabeth not only understood; she was thrilled. 'You are
the most blessed of all women,' she said, 'and blessed is the
child you will bear.'

"As she spoke, I could feel a song bubbling up inside me:

With all my being I praise the Lord,

And every part of me rejoices in God

who always takes care of me.

For I am no one special,

Yet God has noticed me

and is doing good and great things for me.

When my story is told,

all people everywhere will say

that I am blessed.

"I still had problems to solve when I returned home. Joseph was troubled at my news. I was afraid he would not want to marry me. Then, in a dream, an angel spoke to him. From that moment on, he promised to take care of me always.

"So it was that we traveled together to Joseph's home town of Bethlehem, to register our names in the great census ordered in those days by the Roman emperor.

"The place was so full of travelers, we took shelter in a
stable. There, my baby was born. I had swaddling clothes to
wrap him in, but no cradle; so I laid him to sleep in the manger.

"Later that night, strangers came to visit: shepherds, who had
been out watching over their flocks of sheep on the hillside.
Such a tale they told! 'We saw angels,' they said, 'shining with
all the brightness of God.

" 'The angels told us that a baby had been born—the One sent by God to save our people and to bring joy to all the world. And here is the baby, just as they said.'

"In my heart, I knew more than ever that what the angel had told me had to be true.

"A few weeks later we took Jesus to the Temple in the great
city of Jerusalem, which lies just a little way from Bethlehem.
We wanted to give thanks to God for the baby's safe arrival,
following the customs of our people.

"An old man named Simeon came to greet us. As he held the
baby, his eyes shone with joy. 'This is God's special One,' he
said. 'I shall die happy now that I have seen him.'

"Then he spoke to me—words I never forgot. 'This baby will bring the world joy,' he said. 'But there will be troubles too, and sorrow that will pierce your heart like a sharp sword.'

"Later, more visitors came to visit us in Bethlehem: men who were both wealthy and wise. They told us they had seen a new star, and they believed it was sign that a great king had been born. They had followed the star from lands far to the east to come to our little family. They gave rich gifts for the baby— gold, frankincense and precious myrrh.

"But the travelers had set people gossiping, and in Jerusalem, our wicked king Herod had heard the rumors. He wanted to kill any baby king... so God gave Joseph a special dream that warned him to flee for our lives. We went together, in the dark of night, to distant Egypt.

"With God's help, we kept Jesus safe till the wicked king was dead, and at last we returned to Nazareth. I remember how fast Jesus grew up. Soon he was as tall as any of you are now!

"When he was nearly a man, we took him to Jerusalem to celebrate the great festival called Passover at the Temple there. As we journeyed home with others from Galilee, we realized he was not with us.

"I was desperately anxious. Three days I searched, and every night I lay awake worrying for my boy. What could have happened?

"At last we found him, talking with the wise teachers in the Temple. 'Why did you have to look so hard for me?' he asked. 'Didn't you know I had to be in my Father's house?'

"Ah yes: the angel had said Jesus was God's Son; no wonder he called God 'Father.'

"When Jesus was a grown man, he left his home in Nazareth. He began to call people to live as friends of God. He called men and women as they went about their work, and children as they played. People could understand his message, for he was himself a friend to all.

"I watched Jesus welcome everyone into his family... into God's family... by telling stories and working miracles.

"One day, at a wedding, there was not enough wine. The family was so embarrassed! I asked Jesus to help them. I was a little afraid he might not, especially when he asked the servants to fetch great jars of water. But as the water was poured, it turned to wine. And it was the very best.

"Yet, though he did good things, some people grew to hate Jesus. Among them were some of the religious leaders of our people, who had given their lives to studying and trying to understand what God is like. I think they were jealous of Jesus, who seemed so confident of God's love and forgiveness, and who worked miracles of healing in God's name.

"Together they plotted. They had him put on trial as a criminal. They told such lies that he was condemned to die.

"I watched, weeping, as soldiers nailed him to a cross of wood. I watched as he hung dying. I looked into his sad eyes, and he saw me. By my side stood his good friend, John, and he asked John to take care of me always.

"I was weeping still as Jesus breathed his last. I was weeping as men took the body down and a good, kind man arranged for it to be put in a stone tomb. In the midst of my sorrow, I remembered that this had been foretold. And my heart felt cold inside, colder than a stone tomb in bleakest winter.

"For every winter, there is a spring, when new leaves unfurl, fresh and green. Much more wonderful was the spring morning, three days after we laid Jesus' body in the tomb. The stone door was rolled open; Jesus' body had gone. By a miracle, he was alive!

"He met with his friends and spoke with them. He showed us that death was not the end. He said that those that follow in the way he taught can live as sons and daughters of God for ever. He wanted us to tell that news to everyone, for he was going to God in heaven.

"I have been with Jesus' followers ever since, doing as Jesus said. God's own Holy Spirit helps us in our task. We started in Jerusalem, and the news is spreading to all the world."

"What do people have to do to live as friends of God?" asked one child. Mary looked toward John, the friend of Jesus who had always taken care of her since Jesus died.

"John has put it like this," she said: " 'Little children, let us love one another, not just in what we say but what we do. Let us love one another, because love is from God.' "